Horatio Rogers

Mary Dyer of Rhode Island

The Quaker martyr that was hanged on Boston Common, June 1, 1660

Horatio Rogers

Mary Dyer of Rhode Island
The Quaker martyr that was hanged on Boston Common, June 1, 1660

ISBN/EAN: 9783337403065

Printed in Europe, USA, Canada, Australia, Japan

Cover: Foto ©Andreas Hilbeck / pixelio.de

More available books at **www.hansebooks.com**

MARY DYER

OF RHODE ISLAND

THE QUAKER MARTYR

THAT WAS HANGED ON BOSTON COMMON, JUNE 1, 1660

BY

HORATIO ROGERS

ASSOCIATE JUSTICE OF THE SUPREME COURT
OF RHODE ISLAND

PREFACE

THE interest awakened by a paper read by me last fall before the Rhode Island Historical Society, of which I was then the President, has induced me to revise the matter then used, and to accept the offer of the publishers of this volume to issue it in its present form.

The material for a sketch of Mary Dyer is meagre, and necessarily has to be gathered, bit by bit, from many sources, the principal of which are George Bishop's *New England Judged by the Spirit of the Lord*, Part I., 1661, and Part II., 1667,—both parts, somewhat abbreviated, again printed in 1703: John Whiting's *Truth and Innocency Defended against Falshood and Envy. And the Martyrs of Jesus, and Sufferers for his sake,*

Vindicated, 1702; *A Call from Death to Life,
being an Account of the Sufferings of Marmaduke Stephenson, William Robinson and Mary
Dyer, in New England, in the year* 1659,
printed by Friends in London, 1660, a private
reprint of which was made in 1865, includ-
ing Marmaduke Stephenson's *A Call from
Death to Life*, and other papers, with an
Introduction; Joseph Besse's *A Collection of
the Sufferings of the People called Quakers,*
1753; Sewel's *History of the People called
Quakers;* Bowden's *History of the Society of
Friends in America;* and the *Massachusetts
Records*. In addition to these, however,
many works, too numerous to mention, have
been consulted and drawn from; for the
labor involved in such a study is out of all
proportion to the space occupied by the
narrative.

H. R.

PROVIDENCE, R.I., February, 1896.

Mary Dyer of Rhode Island,

The Quaker Martyr that was Hanged on Boston Common, June 1, 1660.

I

AMONG the most pathetic chapters of New England history are those that recount the sufferings for conscience sake. Every gradation of cruelty known to Puritan persecution was practised upon the Quakers. Many of the victims of this religious intolerance were inhabitants of Rhode Island visiting neighboring colonies, for the hand of persecution could not reach across its border; the government of Rhode Island, in 1657, when urged by the Commissioners of the

United Colonies to expel the Quakers from its boundaries, writing in reply as follows: " And as concerning these quakers (so caled) which are now among us, we have no law among us whereby to punish any for only declaring by words, &c, their mindes and understandings concerning the things and ways of God, as to salvation and an eternal condition." [1]

Massachusetts Bay was the most active of the New England persecutors, but Plymouth Colony and the colonies along the Connecticut River also shared the persecuting spirit. When the Quakers first arrived in Boston Harbor, in 1656, Massachusetts was without legislation specially aimed at the new sect; but lack of legislation did not stand in the way of intolerance, and then, too, the

[1] See Appendix I.

General Court rapidly provided con-
stantly increasing punishment for what
they denominated "the cursed sect of
Quakers," whom they denounced in an
address to the King, in 1660, as "open
and capitall blasphemers, open seducers
from the glorious Trinity, . . . and from
the Holy Scriptures as the rule of life,
open ennemyes of government itself as
established in the hands of any but men
of theire owne principles, . . . and malig-
nant and assiduous promoters of doctrines directly tending to subvert both
our churches and state." The forms of
law were but scantily observed. "You
are court, jury, judge, accusers, wit-
nesses, and all" — said Coddington. The
Puritan ministers were particularly forward in the persecution. The Rev. John
Norton, one of the pastors of the Boston
First Church, was clamorous for the pas-

sage of the law of banishment under penalty of death upon return, and it was his pen that wrote the so-called vindication of the Massachusetts authorities for putting Quakers to death in 1659. The Rev. John Wilson, another of the pastors of the Boston First Church, seemed fairly beside himself as the sad work proceeded. "I would carry fire in one hand," said he, "and fagots in the other, to burn all the Quakers in the world. . . . Hang them," he cried, "or else"—and then he significantly drew his finger across his throat, suggestive of cutting it.

The stocks and the pillory, stripes at the whipping-post or at the tail of an ox-cart, fines and imprisonment, branding and mutilation, banishment and death upon the gallows, were meted out with shocking barbarity to unresisting victims, who exhibited a constancy and a heroism in suffering never surpassed in the history of the world. Many were imprisoned, some for years. Some were reduced from comfort to penury by the fines imposed upon them. Some had their ears cut off, and the law provided for boring the tongue through with a hot iron. Two were ordered to be sold into slavery to pay their fines, and large numbers were mercilessly whipped. Neither age nor sex was spared. William Brend, a man of years, was given " in all One Hundred and Seventeen Blows with a pitch'd Rope, so that his Flesh," in the words of the narrator, " was beaten Black, and as into a Gelly; and under his Arms the bruised Flesh and Blood hung down, clodded as it were in Baggs; and so into One was it beaten that the sign of one particular Blow could not be seen." He was also starved for five days, and for sixteen hours was put into irons, neck and heels, so that it was thought he would die — all of which so excited the populace that the authorities promised that the jailer should be punished, but no further notice was taken of it.

Christopher Holder of Rhode Island was barbarously whipped, was then kept for three days without food or water, and without bed or straw, and for nine weeks was imprisoned without fire in the cold winter season. Afterwards he was apprehended again, was again cruelly whipped, his right ear was cut off, and other barbarities were at different times practised upon him.

Defenceless women, maidens and matrons, were stripped naked to the waist, and, thus exposed to the public gaze,

were beaten with whips of threefold
knotted cord until the blood ran down
their bare backs and bosoms. George
Bishop, the Quaker historian of the
time, whose narrative is couched in the
form of an address to the Massachusetts
General Court, being an answer to an
apologetic declaration issued by the Court
after the hanging of two Quakers in
1659, thus relates the treatment dealt
out to two Rhode Island women in
Boston. "Horred Gardner is the next,"
says Bishop, "who being the Mother of
many Children, and an Inhabitant of
Newport in Rhode Island, came with
her Babe sucking at her Breast, from
thence to Weymouth (a Town in your
Colony) where having finished what she
had to do, and her Testimony from the
Lord, unto which the witness of God
answered in the People, she was hurried

by the baser sort to Boston, before your
Governour, John Endicot, who after he
had entertained her with much abusive
Language, and the Girl that came with
her to help bear her Child, he committed them both to Prison, and Ordered
them to be whipp'd with Ten Lashes
apiece, which was cruelly laid on their
Naked Bodies, with a three-fold-knotted-
Whip of Cords, and then were continued
for the space of Fourteen Days longer
in Prison, from their Friends, who could
not Visit them. The Woman came a
very sore Journey, and (according to
Man) hardly accomplishable, through a
Wilderness of above Sixty Miles, between
Rhode Island and Boston; and being
kept up, after your Cruel Usage of their
Bodies, might have died; but you had
no Consideration of this, or of them, tho'
the Mother had of you, who after the

Savage, Inhumane and Bloody Execution on her, of your Cruelty aforesaid, kneeled down, and Prayed — *The Lord to Forgive you* — which so reached upon a Woman that stood by, and wrought upon her, that she gave Glory to God, and said — *That surely she could not have done that thing, if it had not been by the Spirit of the Lord.*"

The other Rhode Island woman was Catharine Scott, an ancestress of the author, and a sister of the famous Mrs. Anne Hutchinson. She went to Boston to be near a young friend of hers in his sufferings, Christopher Holder, already alluded to, who afterwards married her daughter. Of her, Bishop thus writes: "And Katharine Scot, of the Town of Providence, in the Jurisdiction of Rhode-Island (a Mother of many Children, one that had lived with her

Husband, of an Unblameable Conver-
sation, and a Grave, Sober, Ancient
Woman, and of good Breeding, as to
the Outward, as Men account) coming
to see the Execution of the said Three,
as aforesaid, whose Ears you cut off,
and saying upon their doing it pri-
vately, — *That it was evident they were
going to act the Works of Darkness, or
else they would have brought them forth
Publickly, and have declared their Offence, that others may hear and fear.* —
Ye committed her to Prison, and gave
her Ten Cruel Stripes with a three-fold-
corded-knotted-Whip, with that Cruelty
in the Execution, as to others, on the
second Day of the eighth Month, 1658.
Tho' ye confessed, when ye had her
before you, that for *ought ye knew,
she had been of an Unblameable Conver-
sation;* and tho' some of you knew

her Father, and called him Mr. Marbery, and that she had been well-bred (as among Men) and had so lived, and that she was the Mother of many Children; yet ye whipp'd her for all that, and moreover told her, — *That ye were likely to have a Law to Hang her, if she came thither again.* To which she answered, — *If God call us, Wo be to us, if we come not; And I question not, but he whom we love, will make us not to count our Lives dear unto ourselves for the sake of his Name.* To which your Governour, John Endicot, replied — *And we shall be as ready to take away your Lives, as ye shall be to lay them down.*" [1]

[1] The Scott family were staunch Quakers and very friendly with Mary Dyer. One of the daughters, Patience, when only eleven years old, was imprisoned in Boston with Mary Dyer when the latter was ban-

To thoroughly comprehend the religious situation in New England at the
time of these persecutions, and the spirit
actuating both persecutors and victims,
it is necessary to bear in mind the
environments of those times, and to
breathe the atmosphere, so to speak,
then pervading society. The sensuous
splendor and formalism that character-
ized the worship of the Romish Church,
and the extravagant indulgences allowed its members, resulted in the re-

ished from Massachusetts. Another daughter, Mary,
who afterwards married Christopher Holder, was imprisoned in Boston with Mary Dyer when the latter
returned there and met her death, Mary Scott being
allowed to return home after having been admonished
by the General Court. Still another daughter, Hannah
Scott, married Walter Clarke, a strong Quaker and for
a number of years Governor of Rhode Island, and it is
from her that the author is descended. Mrs. Catharine
Scott's father was the Rev. Francis Marbury of London, and her mother was a sister of Sir Erasmus
Dryden, Bart., grandfather of John Dryden the poet.

ligious revolt in the sixteenth century
known as the Protestant Reformation.
The reforming spirit, when once awakened, is difficult to hold in check, and,
as decade succeeded decade, new re-
formers sought to reform former refor-
mations, until in a few score years
the Lutheran and Anglican Churches
seemed conservative indeed, and a large
religious party of heterogeneous ele-
ments easy to fall apart, sprang up in
England known as Puritans, which, as
the name implied, desired to purify the
reformed churches. Aught suggestive
of Rome or Romish faith or forms,
was an object of Puritan abomination.
Uniformity of worship among Protes-
tants became impossible, as each shade
of belief, while advocating uniformity,
insisted that all should conform to their
particular tenets, and, until liberty of

conscience was established whereby every one was free to judge and act for himself in matters of religion, cruelty and oppression were exercised by those of the ascendant faith towards those not in accord with their views.

In order to enjoy greater toleration, a considerable number of Puritans removed from England to Holland, where they formed churches of their own; but, in course of time, not relishing the manners of the Dutch, they emigrated to America and settled at Plymouth. From time to time numbers who found strict conformity to the Church of England irksome, came to America, and in 1630 Massachusetts Bay was settled, the colonies on the Connecticut River being settled a few years later. Massachusetts Bay, though not the earliest of the New England colonies, became at once from its settlement the leading and representative Puritan colony, and to it reference is almost exclusively made in this volume when Puritan thought and social manners here in America are alluded to.

In Massachusetts Bay, Church and State were firmly united, and only members of the church were admitted as freemen. The Puritan ministers were looked up to by the legislators, and were called upon to frame laws. They were also called to sit in council and give advice in matters of religion and cases of conscience which came before the General Court, and without them the Court never proceeded to any act of an ecclesiastical nature. Religion was the absorbing question of the times. The Rev. Francis Higginson, in his Election Sermon in 1663, said: "It

concerneth New England always to re-
member, that they are originally a plantation religious, not a plantation of
trade. The profession of the purity of
doctrine, worship and discipline is written
upon her forehead. Let merchants, and
such as are increasing cent per cent re-
member this, that worldly gain was not
the end and design of the people of New
England, but religion." President Oakes
of Harvard College, in his Election Sermon in 1673, in referring to Massachusetts Bay, said, "I look upon this as a
little model of the glorious kingdom of
Christ on earth."

The Puritans made the saving of souls
a dismal, dreary piece of business; for
salvation with them seemed to rest on
abject fear of hell fire and eternal dam-
nation, rather than on the atoning love
of that meek and gentle Saviour who

offered up his life for us on Calvary.
Their sermons extended through hours,
and their prayers were exhaustingly pro-
tracted. People were fined for not attending church and were compelled to
contribute to the support of the ministers. Any infraction of the Sabbath met
with speedy punishment. They were
solemn in appearance, austere in manner,
plain in attire, and grave in speech,
which was interlarded with scriptural
phrases. The Bible, and especially the
books of the Old Testament, they claimed
as their guide, and quaint Old Testament
names were given to their children, one
of Mary Dyer's sons being named Maher-
shallalhashbaz. They were a God-fearing
people and never forgot that there were
souls to be saved, or rather that there
were souls in danger of being damned;
for they seemed never to emerge from

c

the gloom and shadow of fear into the joyous brightness of hope, and hence, by the standards of to-day, their lives were comparatively joyless. As might be expected, their laws were rigorous to the last degree. Not only were immorality and levity, but even many of the innocent enjoyments of life were sternly repressed. Especially were improprieties between the sexes relentlessly punished,[1] and innocent intercourse between them and the advances towards marriage were regulated by law. Women were forbidden to expose their arms or necks to

[1] To such an extreme was this carried, if the date of the birth of a young married couple's first-born indicated any impropriety before marriage, the parents were publicly punished, though they had been married for months.

In the colony of New Haven it was ordered in 1650, "That no master of a familye shall give interteinment or habitation to any young man to sojourne in his familye, but by the allowance of the inhabitants

view, and it was ordered that their
sleeves should reach down to their
wrists, and their gowns should be closed
around their throats. Sumptuary laws
and all other kinds of laws regulating
private conduct were in force. The use
of tobacco was forbidden, and so was
dancing at weddings. In 1659 the
General Court of Massachusetts Bay
passed the following law, viz. : " For
p̄venting disorders arising in severall
places w^{th}in this jurisdicōn, by reason of
some still observing such ffestivalls as
were superstitiously kept in other coun-
trys, to the great dishonour of God and
offence of others, it is therefore ordered

of the towne where he dwells, under the penalty of
twenty shillings per week. And it is allso ordered,
that no young man that is neither married, nor hath
a servant, nor is a publique officer, shall keepe house
by himselfe, without the consent of the towne, for and
under paine or penalty of twenty shillings a week."

by this Court and the authority thereof, that whosoever shall be found observing any such day as Christmas or the like, either by forbearing of labour, feasting, or any other way, uppon any such accounts as aforesajd, every such person so offending shall pay for every such offence five shillings as a fine to the county."

Of course, in a community thus constituted, any divergence from the orthodox standard of religious belief would not be tolerated; and Roger Williams became the first victim of Puritan orthodoxy in 1635, founding the Colony of Providence Plantations the next year upon a basis utterly at variance with President Oakes's "little model of the glorious kingdom of Christ on earth," and which, in the judgment of the world, was a vast improvement upon it.

Within a few years succeeding Roger
Williams's banishment, the Rev. John
Wheelwright, Mrs. Anne Hutchinson,
Samuel Gorton, and many others, were
thrust out of Massachusetts Bay in rapid
succession under varying circumstances
of indignity and cruelty. The Quakers
were the next class of religious victims
to feel the hand of Puritan persecution;
but, peaceful as were their professions,
they were made of sterner stuff than
the preceding victims of Puritan oppression, and, undaunted by either threats or
sufferings, fairly repressed the persecuting spirit by surfeiting it with more
victims courting martyrdom than could
be disposed of. At a time of such a
religious awakening as the middle of the
seventeenth century, and, in the words
of Hildreth, as "one among many other
results of that violent fermentation of

opinions among part of the English
Puritans, which Cromwell, to the hor-
ror of the conservative Presbyterians,
allowed to go on almost unchecked,"
George Fox founded the sect called
Quakers or Friends, Fox beginning his
preaching about the year 1647.

For the leading traits of the Quaker
belief I shall borrow and abridge from
the Quaker writer Hallowell, in his
Quaker Invasion of Massachusetts. In
common with the Puritans, the Quakers
believed in the divinity of Jesus, the
Christian atonement, a future life either
in heaven or hell, and the inspiration
of the Bible. In common with the Puritans, they condemned as idolatrous the
ceremonial service of the Established
Church; but they also denied the efficacy
of ordination, baptism, formal prayer,
and the sacrament of the Lord's Supper.

They sought to restore the spirituality and simplicity of primitive Christianity. Their reliance upon what they called the Inward Light, as a sufficient guide in matters of religion, has always distinguished them from all other religious sects. This Inward Light may be briefly explained as follows : God is an indwelling Spirit, and humanity is his holy temple. His law is written upon the hearts of all men; and obedience to it will lead them into all truth, so far as religious truths are revealed to men. Through the operation of this law the soul of man is accessible to his Creator. It is the rule of life to which every one must subject himself, and out of which duty is evolved. The logic of this cardinal principle of Quakerism led straight to repudiation of the authority of an ordained ministry, to the withdrawal from church membership, and the refusal to pay church tithes. Intellectual training alone cannot fit men to be religious teachers. The Spirit of God must first illuminate their souls and sanctify their lives. The Puritans rebelled against prelacy, and held in special abhorrence the forms and ceremonies borrowed from Rome by the English Church. Coming into power, they established their own church, and compelled an unwilling people to conform to and support it. The Quakers probed deeper. They rebelled against prelate and presbyter alike. They claimed not toleration, but liberty of conscience for all as an inalienable right; they demanded the absolute separation of Church and State, denounced the clergy as priests and hirelings, and in spite of fiendish persecution refused to acknowledge their authority or to contribute so much as a farthing to their maintenance. Silent meditation, interrupted only by a short prayer or exhortation by one or more of them, who, perchance, were moved by the Spirit, constituted their only form of worship. They substituted simple affirmation for the oath, defending the innovation with apt and telling quotations from scripture. They held meetings for worship, and were generally careful to abstain from all unnecessary secular employment on the first day of the week, but they did not regard it as especially the "Lord's Day." They claimed that all days are alike holy in the sight of God. They regarded the use of the plural number in addressing one person as a species of flattery, and adopted the simple *thee* and *thou* of the Bible. They addressed all men by their Christian names only, regarding all other modes of address as " flattering titles." They declared that it is not lawful for Christians to kneel or prostrate themselves to any man, or to bow the body, or to uncover the head to men; that it is not lawful for a Christian to use superfluities in apparel, as are of no use save for ornament and vanity; that it is not lawful to use games, sports, plays, nor, among other things, comedies, among Christians, under the notion of recreations, which do not agree with Christian silence, gravity, and sobriety. They considered war an evil as opposite and contrary to the spirit and doctrine of Christ as light to darkness, and they would not fight.

That injustice may not be done, it should be borne in mind that the persecution of the Quakers in Massachusetts

was the work of the ministers and of
the higher civil magistrates; that but a
portion of the church members, and few,
if any, who were not, approved of it;
that as only church members were freemen and entitled to vote, those in authority were elected by the church
members only; and yet, when the penalty of death was sought to be imposed
upon those who returned from the banishment meted out to the Quakers, the
utmost difficulty was encountered, and
only after a stubborn resistance was the
law enacted by the General Court by a
bare majority of one. Popular tumults
were frequently excited by the treatment
of the Quakers, and, in the case of William Brend already alluded to, we have
seen that the authorities, in order to
allay the popular discontent, had to
promise to bring the jailer to justice, he

having been the instrumentality used in perpetrating the cruelties. It was urged by those in favor of the law that its mere existence, operating *in terrorem*, would be all-sufficient, and that its enforcement would never be necessary. Those stern old Puritans were full of grim determination, and it never entered their heads that their Quaker opponents could be as doggedly tenacious in upholding their views as they were themselves. Certain it is that those Massachusetts lawmakers did not reckon upon the existence of a zeal, a courage, a heroism — call it what you will — that would break down and triumph over their own determination, which was well-nigh relentless. They had never seen a self-sacrifice that conquered by its very submissiveness, and overwhelmed persecutors by a surfeit of victims offering themselves for sacrifice.

The Quakers were absolutely fearless. They counted their lives as nothing in upholding their views, and they not only did not avoid martyrdom, but they studiously courted it; and therein lay their power and the secret of their final triumph.

II

MARY DYER of Rhode Island, in the
words of George Bishop, the old Quaker
chronicler, written after her death, was
"a Comely Grave Woman, and of a
goodly Personage, and one of a good
Report, having a Husband of an Estate,
fearing the Lord, and a Mother of Children." Governor Winthrop of Massachusetts, a less friendly writer, refers to
her, in 1638, as "the wife of one William
Dyer, a milliner in the New Exchange,
a very proper and fair woman, and both
of them notoriously infected with Mrs.
Hutchinson's errors, and very censorious
and troublesome, (she being of a very
proud spirit, and much addicted to revelations)." Gerard Croese, a Dutch writer,

states that she was reputed as a " person of no mean extract and parentage, of an estate pretty plentiful, of a comely stature and countenance, of a piercing knowledge in many things, of a wonderful sweet and pleasant discourse, so fit for great affairs, that she wanted nothing that was manly, except only the name and the sex."

William Dyer and his wife emigrated from London to Boston, in Massachusetts Bay, where they were admitted members of the Rev. Mr. Wilson's church, December 13, 1635. That they were better educated than the majority of people of that day, is apparent from the character of the public positions William Dyer held in Rhode Island, and from the letters of Mrs. Dyer that have come down to us,[1] and the fact that she was a great friend

[1] See Appendix II.

of the gifted Mrs. Anne Hutchinson.
When the latter was arraigned before the
elders and was expelled from the church,
Mary Dyer rose and walked by her side
out of the building. The Dyers followed
the Rev. Mr. Wheelwright and Mrs.
Hutchinson in the Antinomian move-
ment, and in March, 1637, William
Dyer signed a remonstrance affirming
the innocence of Mr. Wheelwright and
that the Court had condemned the truth
of Christ. In consequence of this he
and others of like sympathies were dis-
franchised and disarmed, " because," in
the language of the order, " the opinions and revelations of Mr. Wheelwright and Mrs. Hutchinson have
seduced and led into dangerous errors
many of the people here in New England; " and early in the next year they
were forced to leave Massachusetts,

removing first to Portsmouth, Rhode Island, and the following year to Newport in the same State.

Palfrey, the historian, says that Mary Dyer was an object of peculiar abhorrence in Boston on account of an absurd story of her having given birth to a monster, a divine judgment for her attachment to Mrs. Hutchinson. The story in all its disgusting detail is given by Governor Winthrop in his *History of New England*, and by Cotton Mather in his *Magnalia Christi Americana*.

William Dyer was a person of consequence in Rhode Island. In 1638 he was elected Clerk, and in 1640 Secretary of Portsmouth and Newport, holding the office until May, 1647, and thereafter for a year he was the General Recorder under the Parliamentary Patent. Two years later he was the

Attorney-General of the Colony. At different times he held various other offices and positions of public trust, such as a Commissioner, a Deputy, General Solicitor, Secretary of the Council, etc.

William and Mary Dyer had six children, and among their numerous descendants are some of the best known and most respected citizens of Rhode Island.[1]

[1] William and Mary Dyer's descendants include the late Benjamin Dyer and Charles Dyer, leading merchants in Providence in the early part of this century; the late Elisha Dyer, senior, also prominent there in business; the late Governor Elisha Dyer, who filled with honor the Executive Chair of the State; the late Daniel W. Lyman, to whose munificence Brown University is indebted for the Lyman Gymnasium; General Elisha Dyer, until recently Adjutant-General of the State; Mr. James H. Chace, an extensive cotton manufacturer in Providence: the Hon. Jonathan Chace, formerly a United States Senator from Rhode Island; and many others too numerous to mention.

In 1652 William Dyer accompanied
Roger Williams and John Clarke, who
were sent from Rhode Island to England to obtain a revocation of the
extraordinary powers granted to William Coddington; and Mrs. Dyer
accompanied her husband. Though
William Dyer returned home early in
1653, his wife remained abroad several years longer, becoming a convert
to Quaker doctrines and a minister in
that society. In 1657 she landed in
Boston *en route* for her home in Rhode
Island. The year before her coming,
the arrival of the earliest Quakers in
Boston had so wrought up the ministers
and authorities of Massachusetts Bay
that various repressive measures had
been adopted, and hence when Mary
Dyer, and a widow named Ann Burden
who came to settle up her deceased hus-

band's estate, set foot in Boston, they were arrested and cast into prison; for although Mary Dyer's sole business was to pass that way to Rhode Island, she was kept a close prisoner so that none might have communication with her, until her husband, hearing that she had arrived and was in prison, went after her. Then she was not released and suffered to depart until he had bound himself in a great penalty not to lodge her in any town of Massachusetts Bay, nor to permit any to have speech with her on her journey. In 1658 she was expelled from the Colony of New Haven for preaching Quaker doctrines.

As well might the Puritan persecutors of the United Colonies have attempted to stop the inflowing tide of the mighty ocean by their legal fulminations as to curb Quaker zeal by their

cruel enactments, so the victims flocked
on their way to the jails, the whipping posts and the pillories, yea, even
to the gallows.

In June, 1659, William Robinson, a
merchant of London. and Marmaduke
Stephenson, a countryman of the east
part of Yorkshire, 'were moved by the
Lord,' in Quaker phrase, to go from
Rhode Island to Massachusetts to bear
witness against the persecuting spirit
existing there: and with them went
Nicholas Davis of Plymouth Colony,
and Patience Scott of Providence, Rhode
Island, a girl of about eleven years of
age, and a daughter of the Catharine
Scott already referred to. They were
all arrested and committed to prison to
await the next meeting of the Court
of Assistants in the following September. During their incarceration Mary

Dyer was moved of the Lord to go from Rhode Island to visit the prisoners, and she too was arrested and imprisoned. On September 12, 1659, the Court banished the four adults from Massachusetts upon pain of death, if after the 14th of September they should be found within the jurisdiction, but Patience Scott was discharged, as, in the words of the chronicler, "the child, it seems, was not of years, as to law, to deal with her by banishment." [1]

[1] Governor Hutchinson in his *History of Massachusetts*, Vol. I. p. 183, says: "Patience Scott, a girl of about eleven years of age, came I suppose from Providence; her friends lived there; and professing herself to be one of those whom the world in scorn calls quakers, was committed to prison, and afterwards brought to court. The record stands thus: 'The court duly considering the malice of satan and his instruments by all means and ways to propagate error and disturb the truth, and bring in confusion among us — that satan is put to his shifts to make use of such a child, not being of the years of discretion, nor under-

Nicholas Davis and Mary Dyer departed to their homes without the jurisdiction of Massachusetts, but William Robinson and Marmaduke Stephenson, though released from prison, determined to stay within the jurisdiction and try the bloody law unto death. On October 8, within thirty days of her banishment, Mary Dyer with other Rhode Island Quakers went to Boston to visit Christopher Holder, then in prison, where she was again arrested and held for the action of the authorities. Five days later William Robinson and Marmaduke Stephenson, who had

standing the principles of religion — judge meet so far to slight her as a quaker, as only to admonish and instruct her according to her capacity, and so discharge her, Capt. Hutchinson undertaking to send her home.' Strange such a child should be imprisoned! it would have been horrible if there had been any further severity."

been travelling about spreading their doctrines through Massachusetts and Rhode Island since their release from prison, also went to Boston to look the bloody laws in the face, in the words of the Quaker chronicler; and they too were arrested and cast into prison.

The issue was now clearly made between Quaker and Puritan. The Quaker defied the unjust Puritan laws, and dared martyrdom. Dare the Puritan authorities inflict it?

On October 19 the three prisoners were brought before Governor Endicott and the Assistants, and demand having been made of them — Why they came again into that jurisdiction after having been banished from it upon pain of death if they returned? — they severally declared that the cause of their coming was of the Lord and in obedience to him. The next day they were again brought before the magistrates. when the Governor called to the keeper of the prison to pull off their hats, which having been done, he addressed them substantially as follows: "We have made many laws and endeavored in several ways to keep you from among us, but neither whipping nor imprisonment, nor cutting off ears, nor banishment upon pain of death, will keep you from among us. We desire not your death." Notwithstanding which, he immediately added: "Hearken now to your sentence of death." Then he stopped: whereupon William Robinson desired to read to the magistrates and the large audience assembled there a paper prepared by him, containing a declaration of his call by the Lord to Boston and the reason of his staying within the jurisdiction

after his banishment. The Governor
with much feeling said : " You shall not
read it, nor will the court hear it read."
Upon its being passed to the Governor,
and read by him to himself, he said:
" William Robinson, you need not keep
such an ado to have it read, for ye spake
yesterday more than is here written."
To which Robinson replied, " Nay," and
desired again that it might be read, that
all the people might hear the cause of
their coming and of their stay there,
and wherefore they were put to death.
But the Governor would not allow him
to read it, and proceeded to pronounce
sentence of death upon him, whereupon
he was carried back to prison. Then
the Governor addressed Marmaduke
Stephenson, and, more partial to him,
apparently, than to William Robinson,
said, " If you have anything to say,

you may speak." But Stephenson was silent, and spoke not, so sentence of death was pronounced upon him also. When the Governor ceased speaking, however, Stephenson lifted up his voice in this wise: " Give ear, ye magistrates, and all who are guilty, for this the Lord hath said concerning you, who will perform his promise upon you, that the same day that you put his servants to death shall the day of your visitation pass over your heads, and you shall be cursed forevermore, the Lord of Hosts hath spoken it; therefore in love to you all take warning before it be too late, that so the curse might be removed; for assuredly if you put us to death, you will bring innocent blood upon your own heads, and swift destruction will come upon you:" whereupon he, too, was sent back to jail.

Then Mary Dyer was brought to the
bar of the Court, and the Governor pronounced sentence upon her as follows:
"Mary Dyer, you shall go from hence
to the place from whence you came,
and from thence to the place of execution, and there be hanged till you be
dead." To which she said, "The will
of the Lord be done." — "Take her
away, Marshal," quoth the Governor.
She replied, "Yea, and joyfully I go."
And on her way to prison she used simi-
lar words, with praises to the Lord. To
the marshal who had her in custody,
she said, "Let me alone, for I should
go to prison without you." — "I believe
you, Mrs. Dyer," he rejoined, "but I
must do what I am commanded."

Great influence was brought to bear to
prevent the execution of the sentences.
Governor Winthrop of Connecticut ap-

peared before the Massachusetts authorities, urging that the condemned be not
put to death. He said that he would
beg it of them on his bare knees that
they would not do it. Colonel Temple [1]
also addressed the authorities, and said
that if according to their declarations
they desired the prisoners' lives absent
rather than their deaths present, he
would beg them of the authorities, and
would carry them away at his own
charge, and give them a house to live
in, and corn to feed on, and land for
them and their heirs to plant on, that
so once within a year they should be

[1] The proceedings of the General Court of Massachusetts for October 19, 1658 (*Records of Mass.*, Vol. IV.
Part I. p. 355), show that "the honourable Colonell
Thomas Temple is, by cōmission from his highness
the Lord Protector, constituted governor of Acady
and Nova Scotia, from Mereliquish on the east, to St.
Georges and Musconcus on the confines of New England, on the west."

able to provide for themselves; and if any of them should come hither again, he would again fetch them at his own charge. Governor Endicott, the Rev. John Wilson, and the whole pack of persecutors, however, seemed to thirst for blood; and it was determined that somebody must die.

The 27th of October, 1659, was fixed for the triple execution, and elaborate preparations, for those days, were made for it. Popular excitement ran high, and the people resorted to the prison windows to hold communication with the condemned, so the male prisoners were put in irons, and a force was detailed, in the words of the order, "to watch with great care the towne, especially the prison." Captain James Oliver was ordered to detail one hundred soldiers "proportionably out of each company in Boston, completely armed with pike, and musketeers with powder and bullet," to escort the prisoners to the place of execution; though subsequently the order was modified so that thirty-six of the soldiers were to remain in and about the town, while the rest went to the place of execution.

The eventful day having arrived, Captain Oliver and his military guard attended to receive the prisoners. The marshal and the jailer brought them forth, the men from the jail, and Mary Dyer from the House of Correction. They parted from their friends at the prison full of joy, thanking the Lord that he accounted them worthy to suffer for his name and had kept them faithful to the end. The condemned came forth hand in hand, Mary Dyer between the other two, and when the marshal asked her, "Whether she was not ashamed to walk hand in hand between two young men," for her companions were much younger than she, she replied, "It is an hour of the greatest joy I can enjoy in this world. No eye can see, no ear can hear, no tongue can speak, no heart can understand, the sweet incomes and refreshings of the spirit of the Lord which now I enjoy." The concourse of people was immense, the guard was strong and strict, and when the prisoners sought to speak the drums were caused to be beaten.

The method of execution was extremely simple in those days. A great elm upon Boston Common constituted the gallows. The halter having been adjusted round the prisoner's neck, he was forced to ascend a ladder affording an approach to the limb to be used for the fatal purpose, to which limb the other end of the halter was attached. Then the ladder was pulled away, and the execution, though rude, was complete.

Having arrived at the place of execution,[1] the Rev. Mr. Wilson tauntingly said to the prisoners, "Shall such Jacks as you, come in before authority with your Hats on?" To which Robinson replied, "Mind you, mind you, it is for not putting off the Hat we are put to Death." The prisoners took a tender leave of one another, and William Robinson, who was the first to suffer, said, as he was about to be turned off by

[1] Peleg W. Chandler, writing in 1841, in Chandler's *Criminal Trials*, Vol. I., p. 44, note, says in regard to the execution of the Quakers: "These executions are supposed to have taken place on Boston Common, probably near where the Hollis Street Church now stands."

E

the executioner, " I suffer for Christ, in
whom I lived, and for whom I die."
Marmaduke Stephenson came next, and,
being on the ladder, he said to the
people, " Be it known unto all this day,
that we suffer not as evil-doers, but for
conscience sake." Next came Mary
Dyer's turn. Expecting immediate
death, she had been forced to wait at
the foot of the fatal tree, with a rope
about her neck, and witness the violent taking off of her friends. With
their lifeless bodies hanging before her,
she was made ready to be suspended
beside them. Her arms and legs were
bound, and her skirts secured about her
feet; her face was covered with a hand-
kerchief which the Rev. Mr. Wilson,
who had been her pastor when she lived
in Boston, had loaned the hangman.
And there, made ready for death, with

the halter round her neck, she stood upon the fatal ladder in calm serenity, expecting to die. Human devices to arouse terror and to break her spirit had failed. She stood there on that grim height, gazing backward, as it were, upon time, and forward into eternity, without a tremor. In another moment her life would be like a tale that is told. Just then an order for a reprieve, upon the petition of her son all unknown to her, arrives. The halter is loosed from her neck and she is unbound and told to come down the ladder. She neither answered nor moved. In the words of the Quaker chronicler, "she was waiting on the Lord to know his pleasure in so sudden a change, having given herself up to dye." The people cried, "Pull her down." So earnest were they that she tried to prevail upon them to wait a little whilst she might consider and know of the Lord what to do. The people were pulling her and the ladder down together, when they were stopped, and the marshal took her down in his arms, and she was carried back to prison.

All this dismal spectacle made by the authorities, of Mary Dyer, on the 27th of October, 1659, was but a cold-blooded refinement of cruelty to shake her constancy and overcome her fortitude. It was a mere prearranged scheme, for before she set forth from the prison it had been determined that she was not to be executed, as shown by the reprieve itself, which reads as follows: "Whereas Mary Dyer is condemned by the Generall Court to be executed for hir offences, on the petition of William

Dier, hir sonne, it is ordered that the sajd Mary Dyer shall have liberty for forty-eight howers after this day to depart out of this jurisdiction, after which tjme, being found therein, she is forthwith to be executed, and in the meane time that she be kept a close prisoner till hir sonne or some other be ready to carry hir away wthin the afore-sajd tyme; and it is further ordered, that she shall be carrjed to the place of execution, and there to stand upon the gallowes, with a rope about her necke, till the rest be executed, and then to returne to the prison and re-majne as aforesajd."

Evidently her Puritan persecutors did not know Mary Dyer. When she returned to prison and understood the ground of the reprieve, she refused it, and the next morning she wrote to the

General Court, again refusing to accept
her life from her persecutors. She said:
"My life is not accepted, neither availeth me, in comparison with the lives
and liberty of the Truth and Servants
of the living God, for which in the
Bowels of Love and Meekness I sought
you; yet nevertheless with wicked
Hands have you put two of them to
Death, which makes me to feel that
the Mercies of the Wicked is cruelty;
I rather chuse to Dye than to live, as
from you, as Guilty of their Innocent
Blood."

Such constancy and courage as the
prisoners had displayed greatly excited
the populace against the authorities,
who were in a quandary what to do
with Mary Dyer; for as the reprieve
had been kept secret, neither young
William Dyer nor any one else had ap-

peared to take charge of his mother;
so the day after the execution some
officials came and took her in their
arms and set her on horseback and
conveyed her fifteen miles towards
Rhode Island and left her with a horse
and man to be conveyed further. Popular indignation was both loud and
deep. So pronounced was it that the
authorities deemed it necessary to put
forth a declaration in vindication of
their course, or rather, it would seem,
an apology; for such reprehensible and
indefensible conduct could not be vindicated, and it is in answer to that apology that George Bishop wrote his book,
to which I have already referred. Particularly did the Massachusetts authorities claim credit for their reprieve of
Mary Dyer, and ingeniously and indus-
triously did they seek to soften the

judgment of men upon the martyrdom
of Robinson and Stephenson, by vaunt-
ing the consideration they claimed to
have shown Mary Dyer — an argument
which we shall see reacted upon them
when we come to note its effect upon
the recipient of the boasted clemency.

Mary Dyer went to Rhode Island,
where she did not tarry long, as she
spent most of the winter on Long Island.
Terribly in earnest was she; and her
sufferings in no wise abated her purpose
to combat, even unto death, the wicked
persecution taking place in Massachusetts. She was especially roused at the
attempt to vindicate the execution of
Robinson and Stephenson; and the clemency extended to her she believed to be
a mere device to divert, in a measure,
popular indignation. She therefore determined to go again to Boston, and

again defy the authorities, forcing them either to practically annul their unjust laws, if they did not proceed against her, or else by her death to awaken popular indignation that would compel the repeal of them. She arrived in Boston May 21, 1660, and ten days later she was brought before the magistrates. "Are you the same Mary Dyer," inquired Governor Endicott, "that was here before?" — "I am the same Mary Dyer that was here the last General Court," she undauntedly replied. "You will own yourself a Quaker," the Governor inquired, "will you not?" — "I own myself to be reproachfully so called," responded Mary Dyer.[1] Then

[1] W. M. Ferriss, in the article on "Friends" in the *American Cyclopædia*, says: "They soon adopted the name of 'the Religious Society of Friends,' by which they are always known among themselves. The origin of the name Quaker is not entirely certain. By some

the Governor said, "Sentence was passed
upon you the last General Court; and
now likewise — You must return to the
prison, and there remain till to-morrow
at nine o'clock; then thence you must
go to the gallows, and there be hanged
till you are dead." Mary Dyer replied,
" This is no more than what thou saidst
before." — "But now," said the Governor, "it is to be executed. Therefore
prepare yourself to-morrow at nine
o'clock." Then she spoke thus: "I
came in obedience to the will of God

it is affirmed that it was given 'in derision, because
they often trembled under an awful sense of the
infinite purity and majesty of God.' By others it is
said that it was first applied to them in 1650, when
George Fox was brought before the magistrates of
Derby, and he having told them to 'quake at the
name of the Lord,' one of them, Gervase Bennet, an
Independent, caught up the word, and, says Fox,
'was the first that called us Quakers.' However the
name originated, it soon became the one by which
they were generally known in all parts of the world."

the last General Court, desiring you to repeal your unrighteous laws of banishment on pain of death; and that same is my work now, and earnest request, although I told you that if you refused to repeal them, the Lord would send others of his servants to witness against them." Whereupon the Governor sneeringly inquired if she was a prophetess? To which she replied, she spoke the words the Lord spoke in her; and now the thing was come to pass. She then proceeded to speak of her call, when the Governor cried, " Away with her! away with her!" And she was taken back to jail. Her husband, who was not a Quaker, and did not share her views, wrote a letter of earnest intercession for his wife's life to Governor Endicott, but in vain.[1]

[1] See Appendix III.

On June 1, 1660, at nine o'clock, Mary Dyer again set out from the jail for the gallows on Boston Common, surrounded by a strong military guard. As she stood upon the fatal ladder, she was told if she would return home, she might come down and save her life. "Nay," she replied, "I cannot; for in obedience to the will of the Lord God I came, and in his will I abide faithful to the death." Captain John Webb, the commander of the military, said to her that she had been there before, and had the sentence of banishment on pain of death, and had broken the law in coming again now, as well as formerly, and therefore she was guilty of her own blood. "Nay," she replied, "I came to keep blood-guiltiness from you, desiring you to repeal the unrighteous and unjust law of banishment upon pain of death, made against the innocent servants of the Lord, therefore my blood will be required at your hands who wilfully do it; but for those that do it in the simplicity of their hearts, I do desire the Lord to forgive them. I came to do the will of my Father, and in obedience to his will I stand even to the death." Then her old Puritan pastor, the Rev. Mr. Wilson, bade her repent, and be not so deluded and carried away by the deceit of the devil. To which she replied, "Nay, man, I am not now to repent." Being asked whether she would have the Elders pray for her, she replied, "I know never an Elder here." They asked whether she would have any of the people pray for her? She responded, "I desire the prayers of all the people of God." Some scoffingly said, "It may be she thinks there are none here." Looking about, she said, "I know but few here." Then they spoke to her again, that one of the Elders might pray for her. She replied, " Nay, first a child, then a young man, then a strong man, before an Elder of Christ Jesus." And more she spake of the eternal happiness into which she was about to enter; and then, without tremor or trepidation, she was swung off, and the crown of martyrdom descended upon her head. Thus died brave Mary Dyer.[1] Her remains were buried on Boston Common, and there they now rest in an unknown grave.

---

[1] Dr. Snow, in his *History of Boston*, p. 198, says : " One of the officers under the gallows at the time of her execution, Edward Wanton, was so affected at the sight, that he became a convert to the cause of the Friends." The same writer informs us that Wanton was arrested on May 4, 1664, for holding a Quaker meeting at his house in Boston.

In the Friends' Records of Portsmouth, Rhode Island, is this entry: " Mary Dyer the wife of William Dyer of Newport in Rhode Island: She was put to death at the Town of Boston with y^c like cruil hand as the martyrs were in Queen Mary's time, and there buried upon y^c 31 day of y^c 3^d mo. 1660." It will be observed there is an error of a day in the date.

Mary Dyer's Puritan persecutors, strange to say, have found many apologists whose excuses are flimsy indeed. Had her persecutors been Romish priests instead of Puritan ministers and magistrates, such apologists, it is believed, would entertain different views. The persecutions of the Quakers were purely religious and were by no means confined to those who were guilty of improprieties of manner or conduct. Some of the worthiest inhabitants of Massachusetts were cruelly punished for affording the Quakers shelter, or giving them food, or attending their meetings, and even for merely deprecating the inhumanities practised upon them. There was nothing in Quaker doctrine or practice inherently difficult to get on with. If Rhode Island found no difficulty in enduring the Quakers, why could not the other New England Colonies endure them just as well?

The Puritan persecutors themselves said that Mary Dyer was guilty of her own blood. Human rights were nothing to them when their purposes were crossed, and they wondered at a heroism they could not understand, and which was ready to face death, if need be, in the struggle with oppression. The horrible persecutions themselves produced the martyrs. Men's minds were wrought up to the highest pitch, and some were so roused that they were willing to die to put down such wrongs. The feeling is well illustrated by the woman who, in 1658, at the sight of the cruel and bloody infliction of thirty-three stripes each upon two Quakers, at Barnstable, with a three-corded knotted whip, cried out in the grief and anguish of her spirit: "How long, O Lord, how long shall it be ere thou avenge the blood of thine elect?" And afterwards in her bewailings she cried: "Did I forsake father and mother and all my dear relatives to come to New England for this? Did I ever think that New England would come to this? Who would have thought it?"

Mary Dyer did not die in vain. But

F

one more Quaker was executed,[1] and then the torrent of public indignation made itself effectually felt. Governor Endicott stormed and raved at his brother-magistrates for what he deemed their weakness, but it was all in vain; for they would not further imbrue their hands in human blood for such a cause, and even if they would the King sent over to forbid it, ordering the Quakers to be sent to England for trial and punishment. Though the royal order was subsequently modified, and persecution began again and continued for nearly twenty years, yet it went on only intermittently and with decreasing severity until it ceased altogether.[2]

[1] William Leddra, the last Quaker martyr to suffer death in Massachusetts, was hung on Boston Common March 14, 1661.

[2] See Appendix IV.

Roger Williams, the great apostle of
Soul-Liberty, was thrust out of Massachusetts for conscience sake, but Mary
Dyer, a humbler sufferer in the same
great cause, to enable the Heaven-im-
planted principle to obtain root on
Massachusetts soil itself, persisted in
remaining and watering it with her
blood, and God gave the increase; so
that nowhere on the face of the earth
to-day is liberty of conscience more
free or more highly revered than on
the very spot where, in the words of
General Atherton, one of her persecutors, "Mary Dyer did hang as a flag
for others to take example by."

Each must judge for himself of the
credit due Mary Dyer for her sufferings and death. It is a growing belief
that when, in coming ages, the roll
shall be made up of those whose lives

or deaths contributed to the establish-
ment among men of the immortal principle of liberty of conscience, inscribed
in enduring fame upon it will be found
the name of Mary Dyer.

APPENDICES

APPENDIX I

*Letter from the Commissioners of the United
Colonies to Rhode Island, concerning the
Quakers.*

"The Commissioners being Informed that
divers quakers are arrived this summer att
Road Iland, and entertained there which
may prove dangerous to the Collonies,
thought meet to manifest theire minds to
the Governor there as followeth:

"Gent:

"Wee suppose you have understood that
the last yeare a companie of quakers arived
att Boston upon noe other account than to
desperse theire pernisiouse opinions had they
not bene prevented by the prudent care of
that Goverment, whoe by that experience
they had of them being sencable of the

71

Danger that might beefale the Christian Religion heer proffessed, by suffering such to bee Received or continued in the Countrey, presented the same unto the Comissioners att theire meetinge att Plymouth whoe upon that occation comended it to the generall courts of the united Collonies, that all quakers, Rantors, and such notorious heretiques might bee prohibited coming among us and that if such should arise from amongst ourselves speedy care might bee taken to Remove them (and as wee are Informed) the severall Jurisdictions have made provision accordingly; but it is by experience found that means will fall short without further care by Reason of youer Admition and Receiveing of such from whence they may have oppertunitie to creep in amongst us or meanes to enfuse and spred theire Accursed tenates to the great trouble of the Collonies if not to the subversion of the " [lawes] " professed in them; Notwithstanding any care that hath been hitherto taken to prevent the same whereof wee cannot but bee very sencable and thinke noe care to great to preserve us from such a pest the Contagion whereof (if Received) within youer Collonie were dangerous, &c to bee defused to the other by means of the Intercourse, especially to the places of trad amongst us; which wee desire may bee with safety continued between us; Wee therefore make it our Request that you as well as the Rest of the Collonies take such order heerin that youer Naighbours may bee freed from that Danger; That you Remove those Quakers that have been Received, and for the future prohibite theire coming amongst you; whereunto the Rule of Charitie to youer selves and us (wee conceive) doth oblidge you wherin if you should wee hope you will not be wanting: yett wee could not but signify this our Desire; and further declare that wee apprehend that it wil bee our Duty seriously to consider what further provision God may call us to make to prevent the aforsaid mischiefe; and for our further guidance and direction heerin wee desire you to Imparte youer mind and Resolution to the Generall court of the Massachusetts which Assembleth the 14th of October next; wee have not further to trouble you att present but to Assure you wee desire to continew youer loveinge Frinds and Naighbours, the Comissioners of the united Collonie.

" Boston Septem. 12, 1657.

>"Simon Bradstreet, Presedent.
>" Daniel Denison,
>" Thomas Prence,
>" John Mason,
>" John Taylcott,
>" Theophilus Eaton,
>" William Leete."

[Hazard's *State Papers*, Vol. II. p. 370; also *Rhode Island Colonial Records*, Vol. I. p. 374.]

Letter from the Government of the Colony of Rhode Island, in reply to the letter from the Commissioners of the United Colonies, concerning the Quakers.

"Much honoured Gentlemen.

"Please you to understand, that there hath come to our view a letter subscribed by the honour'd gentlemen commissioners of the united coloneys, the contents whereof are a request concerning certayne people called quakers, come among us lately, &c.

"Our desires are, in all things possible, to pursue after and keepe fayre and loveing corespondence and entercourse with all the colloneys and with all our countreymen in New England; and to that purpose we have endeavoured (and shall still endeavour) to answere the desires and requests from all parts of the countrey, coming unto us, in all just and equall returnes, to which end the coloney have made seasonable provision to pre-

serve a just and equal entercourse between
the coloneys and us, by giving justice to
any that demand it among us, and by re-
turning such as make escapes from you, or
from the other coloneys, being such as fly
from the hands of justice, for matters of
crime done or committed amongst you, &c.
And as concerning these quakers (so caled)
which are now among us, we have no law
among us whereby to punish any for only
declaring by words, &c. their mindes and
understandings concerning the things and
ways of God, as to salvation and an eternal
condition.   And we, moreover, finde, that
in those places where these people aforesaid,
in this coloney, are most of all suffered to
declare themselves freely, and are only op-
osed by arguments in discourse, there they
least of all desire to come, and we are informed that they begin to loath this place,
for that they are not opposed by the civill
authority, but with all patience and meek-
nes are suffered to say over their pretended

revelations and admonitions, nor are they
like or able to gain many here to their way;
and surely we find that they delight to be
persecuted by civill powers, and when they
are soe, they are like to gaine more adherents
by the conseyte of their patient sufferings,
than by consent to their pernicious sayings.
And yet we concive, that theire doctrines
tend to very absolute cutting downe and
overturning relations and civill government
among men, if generally received. But as
to the dammage that in likelyhood accrue
to the neighbour colloneys by their being
here entertained, we conceive it will not
prove so dangerous (as else it might) in
regard of the course taken by you to send
them away out of the countrey, as they come
among you. But, however, at present, we
judge it requisitt (and doe intend) to com-
mend the consideration of their extravagant
outgoings unto the generall assembly of
our colloney in March next, where we hope
there will be such order taken, as may, in all

honest and contientious manner, prevent the
bad effects of their doctrines and endeav-
ours; and soe, in all courtious and loving respects, and with desire of all honest and
fayre commerce with you, and the rest of our
honoured and beloved countreymen, we rest

"Yours in all loving respects to serve you,

"Benedict Arnold, Presid.
"William Baulston,
"Randall Howldon,
"Arthur Fenner,
"William Feild.

"From Providence, at the court of tryals,
"held for the coloney, October 13th, 1657.
"To the much honoured, the Generall Court,
"sitting at Boston, for the Colloney of
"Massachusetts."

[Hutchinson's *History of Massachusetts*, Vol. I. Appendix XI. p. 453; also Hazard's *State Papers*, Vol. II.
p. 552; also *Rhode Island Colonial Records*, Vol. I. p.
376.]

*Letter from the General Assembly of the Col-
ony of Providence Plantations to the Massachusetts Bay Colony, in reply to the letter of
the Commissioners concerning the Quakers.*

" Honored Gentlemen :

" There hath beene presented to oure view
by our Honored president, a letter bearing
date September 25th last, subscribed by the
Honoured gentlemen Commissioners of the
United Collonys concerninge a company of
people (lately arrived in these parts of the
world), commonly knowne by the name of
Quakers, whoe are generally conceived pernicious, either intentionally, or at least wise
in efect, even to the corruptinge of good
manners and disturbinge the common peace
and sosieties of the places where they arise
or resort unto, &c.

" Now, whereas, freedom of different consciences, to be protected from inforcements
was the principle ground of our Charter,

both with respect to our humble sute for it, as also to the true intent of the Honourable and renowned parleiment of England in grauntinge of the same unto us; which freedom we still prize as the greatest hapines that men can posess in this world.

"Therefore, we shall for the preservation of our civill peace and order, the more seriously take notice that those people and any other that are here, or shall come amongst us, be impartially required, and to our utmost constrayned to perform all duties requisitt towards the maintaineinge the right of his Highness and the government of that most renowned Parliament of England in this collony, which is most happily included under the same dominion and graciously taken into protection thereof: And in case they the sayd Quakers which are here, or who shall arise or come among us, doe refuse to subject themselves to all duties aforesayed, as trayninge, watchinge, and such other ingadgements, as other members of civill societies, for the preservation of the same in justice and peace; then we determine, yea, and we resolve (however) to take and make use of the first opurtunity to inform our agent residinge in England, that we may humbly present the matter (as touchinge the considerations premised, concerninge the aforenamed people called Quakers) unto the supreame authority of England, humbly craveing their advice and order, how to carry ourselves in any further respect towards these people soe, that therewithall theire may be noe damadge, or infringement of that chiefe principle in our charter concerninge freedom of consciences, and we alsoe are soe much the more incouradged to make our addresses unto the Lord Protector, his highness and government aforesayd; for that we understand there are, or have beine many of the foresayed people suffered to live in England; yea even in the heart of the nation. And thus with our truly thankfull acknowl-

G

edments of the honourable care of the honored gentlemen commissioners of the United Collonies, for the peace and welfare of the whole country, as is expressed in their most friendly letter, we shall at present take leave and rest.

"Yours, most affectionately de-
"sirous of your honors and
"welfaire.

"John Sanford,
"Clerk of the Assembly.

"Portsmouth, March 13th, 1657–8.

"From the General Assembly of the Col-
"lony of Providence Plantations.

"To the much Honored John Endicott,
"Governor of the Massachusetts, to
"be alsoe imparted to the Honorable
"Commissioners of the United Collo-
"nies at their next meeting. These —"

[*Rhode Island Colonial Records*, Vol. I. p. 378.]

Why the authorities of Rhode Island sent *two* letters five months apart, to the General Court of Massachusetts in reply to the letter of the Commissioners of the United Colonies, is inexplicable ; for the letter signed by the Clerk of the General Assembly of Rhode Island evidently refers to the Commissioners' letter of September 12, 1657, notwithstanding the date spoken of in the letter signed by the Clerk, is September 25.

APPENDIX II

Mary Dyer's Letter to the Massachusetts General Court after she had received sentence of death.

"To the General Court now in Boston.

"Whereas I am by many charged with the Guiltiness of my own Blood; if you mean, in my coming to Boston, I am therein clear, and justified by the Lord, in whose Will I came, who will require my Blood of you, be sure, who have made a Law to take away the Lives of the Innocent Servants of God, if they come among you, who are called by you, *Cursed Quakers;* altho' I say, and am a living Witness for them and the Lord, that he hath Blessed them, and

sent them unto you: Therefore be not
found Fighters against God, but let my
Counsel and Request be accepted with you,
To Repeal all such Laws, that the Truth
and Servants of the Lord may have free
Passage among you, and you be kept from
shedding Innocent Blood, which I know
there are many among you would not do,
if they knew it so to be: Nor can the Enemy that stirreth you up thus to destroy
this Holy Seed, in any measure countervail
the great Damage that you will by thus
doing procure: Therefore, seeing the Lord
hath not hid it from me, it lyeth upon me,
in Love to your Souls, thus to persuade
you: I have no self-ends, the Lord know-
eth, for if my Life were freely granted by
you, it would not avail me, nor could I
expect it of you, so long as I should daily
hear or see the Sufferings of these People,
my dear Brethren and Seed, with whom
my Life is bound up, as I have done these
two Years; and now it is like to encrease,

even unto Death, for no evil Doing, but
coming among you: Was ever the like
Laws heard of, among a People that pro-
fess Christ come in the Flesh? And have
such no other Weapons, but such Laws, to
fight against Spiritual Wickedness withall,
as you call it? Wo is me for you! Of
whom take you Counsel? Search with the
Light of Christ in ye, and it will shew you
of whom, as it hath done me and many
more, who have been disobedient and de-
ceived, as now you are; which Light, as
you come into, and obeying what is made
manifest to you therein, you will not Repent, that you were kept from shedding
Blood, tho' it were from a woman: It's not
mine own Life I seek (for I chuse rather
to suffer with the People of God, than to
enjoy the Pleasures of Egypt) but the Life
of the Seed, which I know the Lord hath
Blessed; and therefore seeks the Enemy
thus vehemently the Life thereof to Destroy, as in all Ages he ever did: Oh!

hearken not unto him, I beseech you, for the Seed's sake, which is one in all, and is dear in the sight of God; which they that touch, touch the Apple of his Eye, and cannot escape his Wrath; whereof I having felt, cannot but perswade all Men that I have to do withal, especially you who name the Name of Christ, to depart from such Iniquity, as shedding Blood, even of the Saints of the Most High: Therefore let my Request have as much Acceptance with you (if you be Christians) as Esther had with Ashasuerus (whose Relation is short of that that's between Christians) and my Request is the same that hers was; and he said not, that he had made a Law, and it would be dishonourable for him to Revoke it; but when he understood that these People were so prized by her, and so nearly concerned her (as in Truth these are to me) as you may see what he did for her: Therefore I leave these Lines with you, Appealing to the faithful and true

Witness of God, which is one in all Consciences, before whom we must all appear;
with whom I shall eternally Rest, in ever-
lasting Joy and Peace, whether you will
hear or forbear: With him is my Reward,
with Whom to live is my Joy, and to dye
is my Gain, tho' I had not had your forty
eight Hours warning, for the Preparation
to the Death of Mary Dyar.

"And know this also, That if through the
Enmity you shall declare your selves worse
than Ahasuerus, and confirm your Law, tho'
it were but by taking away the Life of one
of us, That the Lord will overthrow both
your Law and you, by his righteous Judg-
ments and Plagues poured justly upon you,
who now whilst you are warned thereof,
and tenderly sought unto, may avoid the
one, by removing the other: If you neither
hear nor obey the Lord nor his Servants,
yet will he send more of his Servants among
you, so that your end shall be frustrated,
that think to restrain them, you call *Cursed*

Quakers, from coming among you, by any
Thing you can do to them; yea, verily, he
hath a Seed here among you, for whom we
have suffered all this while, and yet Suffer;
whom the Lord of the Harvest will send
forth more Labourers to gather (out of the
Mouths of the Devourers of all sorts) into
his Fold, where he will lead them into fresh
Pastures, even the Paths of Righteousness,
for his Names sake: Oh! let none of you
put this good Day far from you, which verily
in the Light of the Lord I see approaching,
even to many in and about Boston, which
is the bitterest and darkest professing Place,
and so to continue so long as you have
done, that ever I heard of; let the time
past therefore suffice, for such a Profession
as brings forth such Fruits as these Laws
are. In Love and in the Spirit of Meekness
I again beseech you, for I have no Enmity
to the Persons of any; but you shall know,
That God will not be mocked, but what
you sow, that shall you reap from him, that

will render to everyone according to the
Deeds done in the Body, whether Good or
Evil; Even so be it, saith

"MARY DYAR."

"A Copy of this was given to the General
Court after Mary Dyar had received the
Sentence of Death, about the .8th or 9th
Month, 1659."

[Bishop's *New England judged by the Spirit of the
Lord,* 288.]

----

*Mary Dyer's Letter to the Massachusetts Gen-
eral Court, written the day after she was
reprieved on the gallows tree.*

"The 28th of the 8th Month, 1659.

"Once more to the General Court, Assembled in Boston, speaks Mary Dyar, even
as before: My Life is not accepted, neither
availeth me, in Comparison of the Lives
and Liberty of the Truth and Servants of
the living God, for which in the Bowels of

Love and Meekness I sought you; yet nevertheless, with wicked Hands have you put
two of them to Death, which makes me to
feel, that the Mercies of the Wicked is Cruelty; I rather chuse to Dye than to Live,
as from you, as Guilty of their innocent
Blood: Therefore, seeing my Request is
hindred, I leave you to the Righteous Judge,
and Searcher of all Hearts, who, with the
pure measure of Light he hath given to
every Man to profit withal, will in his due
time let you see whose Servants you are,
and of whom you have taken Counsel, which
I desire you to search into: But all his
Counsel hath been slighted, and you would
none of his Reproofs. Read your Portion,
Prov. 1 : 24, to 32. For verily the Night
cometh on you apace, wherein no Man can
Work, in which you shall assuredly fall to
your own Master, in Obedience to the Lord,
whom I serve with my Spirit, and pity to
your Souls, which you neither know nor
pity: I can do no less than once more to

warn you, to put away the Evil of your
Doings, and Kiss the Son, the Light in you,
before his Wrath be kindled in you; for
where it is, nothing without you can help
or deliver you out of his Hand at all; and
if these things be not so, then say, There
hath been no Prophet from the Lord sent
amongst you; though we be nothing, yet
it is his Pleasure, by Things that are not,
to bring to nought Things that are.

" When I heard your last Order read, it
was a disturbance unto me, that was so freely
Offering up my Life to him that gave it
me, and sent me hither so to do, which
Obedience being his own Work, he glori-
ously accompanied with his Presence, and
Peace, and Love in me, in which I rested
from my labour, till by your Order, and the
People, I was so far disturbed, that I could
not retain any more the words thereof,
than that I should return to Prison, and
there remain Forty and Eight Hours; to
which I submitted, finding nothing from

the Lord to the contrary, that I may know
what his Pleasure and Counsel is concerning me, on whom I wait therefore, for he
is my Life, and the length of my Days;
and as I said before, I came at his Command, and go at his Command.

"MARY DYAR."

[Bishop's *New England judged by the Spirit of the
Lord*, 311.]

APPENDIX III

*William Dyer's petition to Governor Endicott
for mercy to his wife.*

" Honor^d S^r

" It is no little greif of mind, and sadness
of hart that I am necessitated to be so
bould as to supplicate yor Honor^d self wth
the Honble Assembly of yor Generall Courte
to extend yor mercy & favoure once agen
to me & my children. Little did I dream
that ever I shuld have had occasion to pe-
titõn you in a matter of this nature, but
so it is that throu the devine providence
and yor benignity my sonn obtayned so
much pitty and mercy att yor hands as to

94

enjoy the life of his mother, now my sup-
plication to yo͏ͬ Hono͏ͬ is to begg affectionately, the life of my deare wife. Tis
true I have not seen her above this half
yeare & therefore cannot tell how in the
frame of her spiritt she was moved thus
againe to runn so great a Hazard to herself, and perplexity to me & mine & all
her freinds & well wishers: so itt is from
Shelter Iland about by Pequid Narragan-
sett & to the Towne of Providence she
secrettly & speedyly journyed, & as secrettly from thence came to yo͏ͬ jurisdiction, unhappy journy may I say, & woe
to that generation say I that gives occasion thus of greif & troble (to thos that
desire to be quiett) by helping one another (as I may say) to Hazard their lives
for I know not whatt end or to what purpose: If her zeale be so greatt as thus
to adventure, oh Lett yo͏ͬ favoure & Pitty
surmount itt & save her life. Lett not
yo͏ͬ forwonted compassion bee conquered by

her inconsiderate madness, & how greatly
will yor renowne be spread if by so con-
quering you become victorious. What shall
I say more. I know you are all sensible
of my condition, and lett the reflect bee,
and you will see whatt my petiton is and
what will give me & mine peace, oh
Lett mercies wings once more sore above
justice ballance, & then whilst I live
shall I exalt yor goodness butt other
wayes twill be a languishing sorrow, yea
so great that I shuld gladly suffer the
blow att once much rather: I shall for-
beare to troble youre Hon^r wth words ney-
ther am I in a capacity to expatiat
myself att present: I only say that yor
selves have been & are or may bee hus-
bands to wife or wives, so am I, yea to
one most dearely beloved: oh do not de-
prive me of her, but I pray give her me
once agen & I shall bee so much obleiged
for ever, that I shall endeavo^r continually
to utter my thankes & render yor Love

& Hon^r most renowned: pitty mee, I begg itt wth teares, and rest yor

"most humbly suppliant

" W DYRE

" Portsm° 27th of 3^d: 1660

"Most Hon^{ed} Sr Lett these lines by yor favo^r bee my Petiton to yor Honble Generall Court: at present Sitting

"sd W D"

[From *Mass. Archives*, X. p. 266 (MSS.).]

u

APPENDIX IV

Duration of the persecution of the Quakers by the Colony of Massachusetts.

Besse, in Vol. II. p. 225, gives the Royal Mandate for the release of the Quakers, as follows : —

" Charles R.

" Trusty and *Welbeloved*, we greet you
" well. Having been informed that several
" of our Subjects among you, called *Quakers*,
" have been and are imprisoned by you,
" whereof some have been executed, and
" others (as hath been represented unto us)
" are in Danger to undergo the Like: We
" have thought fit to signify our Pleasure,
" in that Behalf for the future, and do
" require, that if there be any of those

"People called *Quakers* amongst you, now
"already condemned to suffer Death, or
"other Corporal Punishment, or that are
"imprisoned, or obnoxious to the like Con-
"demnation, you are to forbear to proceed
"any farther, but that you forthwith send
"the said Persons (whether condemned or
"imprisoned) over to this our Kingdom of
"*England*, together with their respective
"Crimes or Offences laid to their charge,
"to the End such Course may be taken
"with them here, as shall be agreeable to
"our Laws, and their Demerits. And for
"so doing, these our Letters shall be your
"sufficient Warrant and Discharge. Given
"at our Court at *Whitehall*, the 9th Day
"of *September* 1661, in the thirteenth Year
"of our Reign.

"Subscribed, *To our Trusty and Welbe-*
"*loved* John Endicot, *Esq: and to all*
"*and every other the* Governour *or* Gov-
"ernours *of our Plantation of* New-Eng-
"land, *and of the Colonies thereunto be-*

" *longing, that now are, or hereafter shall*
" *be :   And to all and every the* Ministers
" *and* Officers *of our said Plantation and*
" *Colonies whatever, within the Continent*
" *of* New-England.

" By His Majesty's Command.

" WIL. MORRIS."

Upon the arrival of the Royal Mandate at Boston the following order was issued : —

" *To* William Salter, *Keeper of the Prison at* Boston.

" You are required, by Authority and Order
" of the General-Court, forthwith to release
" and discharge the *Quakers*, who at pres-
" ent are in your Custody: See that you
" dont neglect this.

" By Order of the Court.

" EDWARD RAWSON, *Secretary.*"

" Boston, the 9th of
" December, 1661."

Hallowell, in his *Quaker Invasion of Massachusetts*, p. 191, says: " A Quaker jubilation followed this gaol delivery, but the liberty they enjoyed was of short duration. Fear of further interference from England having been allayed, the law of May 22, 1661, with slight modification, was reënacted. This was done on the 8th of October, 1662. The fires of persecution were rekindled. John Endicott pursued the Friends with relentless cruelty until, in March, 1665, death ended his wicked and bloody career.

" Bellingham succeeded Endicott, but was less persistent, and instances of cruelty, under his administration, are not numerous. His clemency was due in part to the interference of royal commissioners, who, on the 24th of May, 1665, submitted a series of demands to the General Court, one of which was, that the Quakers should be allowed to attend to their secular business without molestation. Bellingham died in

December, 1672. In November, 1675, persecution was revived by the passage of a
law prohibiting Quaker meetings, and in
May, 1677, it was further provided, that
the constables should 'make diligent search'
for such meetings, and should 'break open
any door where peaceable entrance is denied
them.' For a brief period it seemed as if
the scenes of 1661 and 1662 were to be
reënacted. Men and women were seized,
dragged to gaol, imprisoned, fed on bread
and water, fined, and publicly whipped. In
the 6th month (August) fourteen Quakers
were taken at one meeting, and in the following week a second arrest of fifteen was
made. Most, if not all of them, in addition
to other punishment, suffered flogging at
the whipping post. These are the latest
cases of corporal punishment noted by
Besse. The Friends rallied in increasing
numbers and once more the authorities
were forced to respect their rights."

INDEX

INDEX

I

PUBLICATIONS

OF

PRESTON & ROUNDS,

PROVIDENCE, R.I.

History of the State of Rhode Island and Providence Plantations, 1636-1790.

By SAMUEL GREENE ARNOLD.

New Edition. 2 vols. Octavo. 574 and 600 pp. $7.50, net.

Governor Arnold's History of Rhode Island, based upon a careful study of documents in the British State Paper Office and in the Rhode Island State Archives, supplemented by investigations at Paris and The Hague, has from its publication been the authoritative history of the State.

Genealogical students will find in these volumes the names of over fifteen hundred persons prominent in Rhode Island affairs. This work is of much more than local interest, as the experiment of religious liberty here tried gives to this history an importance far beyond the narrow limits of the State.

"One of the best State histories ever written is S. G. Arnold's History of the State of Rhode Island and Providence Plantations." — JOHN FISKE.

"The best history of Rhode Island is that of Arnold." — PROF. GEORGE P. FISHER, Yale University.

"Mr. Samuel Greene Arnold in his history of Rhode Island has brought together all the extant materials. He brings out more clearly than any previous writer the distinct threads of the previous settlements." — PROF. JOHN A. DOYLE, Oxford.

"A work prepared after long and careful research. Probably no student has ever made himself more familiar with the history of Rhode Island than did Arnold. This work abounds, therefore, in valuable information." — PRES. CHARLES KENDALL ADAMS, Cornell University.

SENT POSTPAID BY THE PUBLISHERS.

Among Rhode Island Wild Flowers.

By W. WHITMAN BAILEY,

Professor of Botany, Brown University.

Cloth. 16mo. Three full-page Illustrations. 75 cents, net.

This admirable little volume, the outgrowth of the author's ripe experience in teaching and in botanizing, contains a popular and interesting account of Rhode Island wild flowers as distributed throughout the State. The favorite collecting grounds are fully described, thus forming a botanical guide to Rhode Island.

In writing this volume Professor Bailey has had in mind the needs of the nature lover, and has discarded technical terms as far as possible, adapting the work to the amateur as well as the botanist.

It should be in the hands of every lover of woodland and meadow.

Forwarded postpaid to any address upon receipt of price by the publishers.

4

Tax Lists of the Town of Providence

During the Administration of Sir Edmund Andros and his Council,

1686–1689.

Compiled by EDWARD FIELD, A.B.,

Member of the Rhode Island Historical Society, and one of the Record Commissioners of the City of Providence.

Cloth. Octavo. 60 pp. $1.00, net.

The " Tax Lists of the Town of Providence " is a compilation of original documents relating to taxation during the Administration of **Sir Edmund Andros and his Council, 1686-1689.** It comprises copies of warrants issued by order of the Council for the assessment and collection of taxes, the tax lists or rate bills prepared pursuant to these warrants, the returns made by the townsmen of their ratable property, and the Tax Laws enacted by Andros and his Council. All of these, with the exception of the laws, are here printed for the first time.

Among the rate bills is the list of polls for 1688, which contains the *names of all males sixteen years of age and upwards living in Providence in August of that year ;* practically a census of the town. For the genealogist and historian this volume contains material of the greatest value on account of the great number of names which these lists contain, besides showing the amount of the tax assessment in each case.

The returns of ratable property form a study by themselves, for they tell in the quaint language of the colonists what they possess, and therefore shed much light on the condition of the times. For a study of this episode in New England Colonial History this work is invaluable.

The index of all names contained in the lists and text is a feature of this work.

The edition is limited to **two hundred and fifty** numbered copies.

Sent postpaid to any address on receipt of one dollar.

5

Early Rhode Island Houses.

An Historical and Architectural Study by NORMAN M. ISHAM, Instructor in Architecture, Brown University, and ALBERT F. BROWN, Architect. Illustrated with a map and over fifty full-page plates. $3.50, net.

No feature in the study of the early life of New England is more valuable or more interesting than the architecture. Nothing throws more light on the home life of the colonists than the knowledge of how they planned and built their dwellings.

Early Rhode Island Houses gives a clear and accurate account of the early buildings and methods of construction, showing the historical development of architecture among the Rhode Island colonists, the striking individuality in the work of the colony and the wide difference between the buildings here and the contemporary dwelling in Massachusetts and Connecticut.

Those interested in colonial life may here look into the early homes of Rhode Island with their cavernous fireplaces and enormous beams. The student will find in these old examples a valuable commentary on New England history, while the architect will discover in the measurements and analyses of construction much of professional interest.

Among the houses described are the Smith Garrison House and the homesteads of the families of Fenner, Olney, Field, Crawford, Waterman, Mowry, Arnold, Whipple, and Manton.

A chapter is devoted to the early houses of Newport, which were unlike those of the northern part of the State and resemble the old work in the Hartford colony.

Photographs and measurements of the dwellings have been made, and from them careful plans, sections, and restorations have been drawn; in some cases six full-page plates admirably drawn and interesting in themselves have been devoted to a single house. Several large plates give illustrations of framing and other details. It is to be noted that these plates are made from measured drawings, that the measurements are given on the plates, and that these constitute in most if not all cases the only exact records for a class of buildings which is destined to disappear at no distant day. It is believed that these drawings, and especially the restorations, will give a clearer idea than has ever before been obtained of the early New England house. A map enables the reader to locate without difficulty the houses mentioned in the text.

The authors have discussed the historical relation of Rhode Island work to contemporary building in the other New England colonies and in the mother country. The book is a mine of authentic information on this subject.

A list of the houses in the State built before 1725, so far as they are known, with dates and a brief description will be found in the appendix.

"This book is probably the most valuable historic architectural treatise that has as yet appeared in America." — *The Nation.*

6

Revolutionary Defences in Rhode Island.

An Historical Account of the Forts and Beacons erected during
the American Revolution.

By EDWARD FIELD, A.B.,

*Past President of the Rhode Island Society of the
Sons of the American Revolution.*

NEARLY READY.

Rhode Island's Adoption of the Federal Constitution.

A Discourse before the Rhode Island Historical Society, at its
Centennial Celebration of Rhode Island's Adoption
of the Federal Constitution.

By HORATIO ROGERS,

President of the Society.

Paper. 44 pp. 8vo. 35 cents, net.

This statement of the reasons which impelled the
state first to hesitate with anxious deliberation, and
afterwards freely and fully to abandon its independent
character, and become an integral part of an indissolu-
ble nation, is made in such form that it should be the
. end of controversy, and the future student of history
should require no further material for a just and dis-
criminating conclusion.

7